This book belongs to

_____

_____

_____

REED

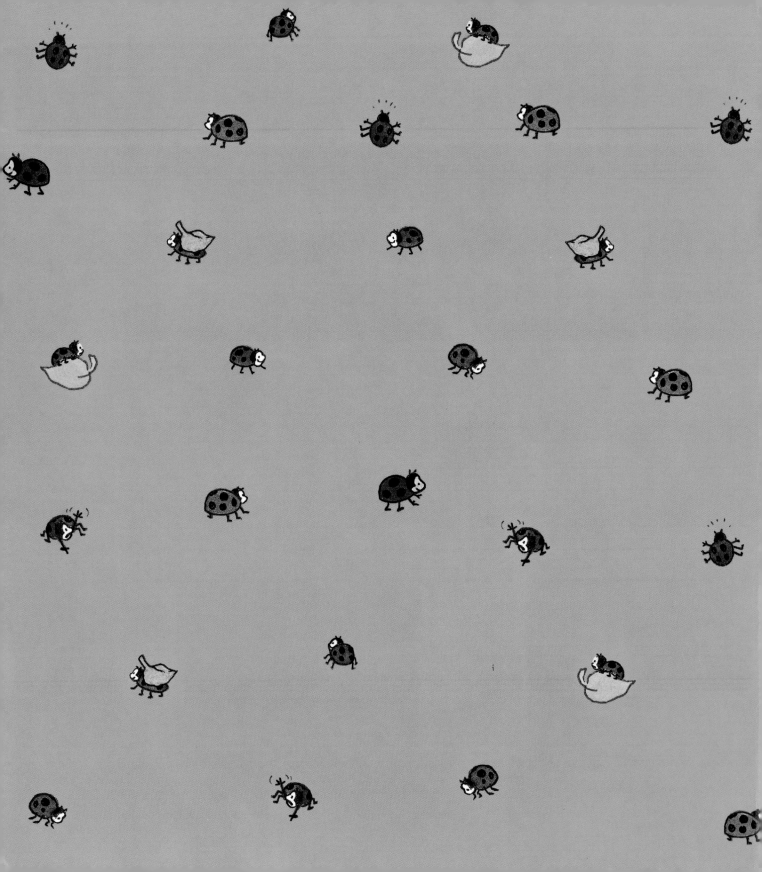

Reed Publishing (NZ) Ltd
Te Karuhi tā tāpui o Reed (Aotearoa)

Established in 1907, Reed is New Zealand's largest
book publisher, with over 300 titles in print.

For details on all these books visit our website:
www.reed.co.nz

Published by Reed Children's Books, a division of Reed Publishing (NZ) Ltd, 39
Rawene Road, Birkenhead, Auckland 10. Associated companies, branches and
representatives throughout the world.

National Library of New Zealand Cataloguing-in-Publication Data

Darroch, Bob, 1940-
Little Kiwi and the dinosaur / written and illustrated by Bob Darroch.
ISBN 1-86948-515-7
[1. Kiwis—Fiction. 2. Weasels—Fiction. 3. Eggs—Fiction.
4. Birds—New Zealand—Fiction] I. Title.
NZ823.2—dc 22

ISBN 1 86948 515 7
First published 2005
Reprinted 2005

Printed in China

Little Kiwi and the Dinosaur

Written and illustrated by
Bob Darroch

REED

Little Kiwi loved his sister. He loved playing games with her, but — well — she was a girl. And girls liked pretty things ... like playing 'nests' and being friends with butterflies ... and being tidy.

He was a 'bloke' and blokes like rough games and exploring and scary things.

'I like scary things too,' argued Little Sister.
'I've got a friend who looks really scary and I
   like **him**!'
But Little Kiwi just laughed.
'How could butterflies be scary?' he chortled.

Still laughing, Little Kiwi wandered off to do 'bloke' things.

Then he saw something frightening: a **weasel**, and he was stealing someone's egg!

Little Kiwi scampered home before he was seen and told his dad.

'Mmm,' thought Dad. 'This is serious. We'll have to warn everyone.'

Later that night all the birds of the forest gathered at the hollow log.

'We'll have to do something,' they decided.

But what?

'We can't peck him — he's too quick.'

'He wouldn't take any notice if we just asked him to leave.'

'We'll have to **scare** him away so that he's too afraid to come back!'

They all agreed with that, but wondered —

'What can we find that's really scary?'

'My friend looks really scary,' whispered Little Sister to her brother.
'Ssh!' he replied.

'We need something like a ... like a dragon,' Dad said.
'My friend is something like a dragon,' Little Sister
   whispered again.
'Be quiet!' her big brother told her.

'... or a dinosaur!' Dad finished.
'My friend is a dinosaur,' Little Sister
   persisted, but her brother ignored her.

'Where can we get a dinosaur?'
   Tui asked.
'I know,' Little Sister
   whispered.
'Go away!' her brother ordered.
   'We're talking about
   important things!'

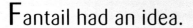Fantail had an idea.

'Let's make one!' she said.

'We can make a pretend dinosaur, one that's so big and scary-looking
    that weasel won't know that it's not real.'

· 'Like this,' she said as she drew her
plan on the ground.
'And we can hide under it and leap
up when weasel comes by!'

'That's a great idea,' Kiwi said. 'We can put some eggs here that
   he'll come to steal and then ... we'll frighten him clean away!'
'This is a great idea,' all the birds agreed, and they flew off to
   gather what they needed.
'Oh yes, a great idea,' chortled someone the birds hadn't seen.
And there was weasel, hiding in the hollow log.

For the rest of the night and all the next day
the birds worked, bending, snapping,

twisting and
knitting sticks,
leaves and moss
into place.

'This is going to be soooo cool,' twittered the waxeyes.
'I'm going to be soooo scared,' giggled weasel, still in his hiding place.

'It won't scare **me**,' muttered Little Sister.
'My friend would be much scarier!'
'Mind your own business,' her brother replied.

It was soon time for testing.
  With the birds inside, the dinosaur reared up,
    waving, chomping, growling and screeching.
  It was frightening!
  'That's going to scare the whiskers off old
    weasel,' Little Kiwi laughed.

'Silly chooks,' mumbled Little Sister
as she wandered away.
'It doesn't scare me!'

All was ready.
The birds put some eggs in the nearby nest
and then hid behind the hollow log.
And waited ...

... but not for long.

Weasel quietly slinked out of the far end of the log,
   right behind the birds.

Before anyone knew he was there he crept up behind
   them and asked, 'Waiting for someone?'

Panic!

The 'dinosaur' exploded in a cloud of screaming, squawking, flapping, panic-stricken birds.

Sticks, feathers, moss and eggshells flew everywhere!

Weasel laughed and laughed, but as he went to pick up the eggs ...
'Get away from them!' boomed a large and terrifying voice from behind some bushes.

A head appeared, a scaly, wrinkled head with spikes on top and fiery eyes.
A dinosaur!
A **real** dinosaur!

It was too much for weasel.
'I'm going, I'm going!' he shrieked and took off into the forest.

From his spot in the wreckage Little Kiwi stayed very still and cautiously peered out.

The weasel had gone but was this dinosaur just as dangerous?

'Well, that's got rid of him!' the dinosaur smiled as he came out from behind the bushes.

'Th ... th ... thanks,' stammered Little Kiwi.

'But — where did you come from?'

'My friend invited me,' the dinosaur told him. 'Here she comes now ...'

'Hello, bro!' said Little Sister. 'Meet my friend Tuatara, the one I was trying to tell you about.'

'Yes, he's a **real** dinosaur,' Little Sister told the birds as, one by one, they returned.

'He can look really mean when he wants to,' she added.

'But I don't want to very often,' said Tuatara.

'We're glad about that,' said the birds as they crowded around to meet and thank him.

Little Kiwi looked proudly at Little Sister.

'Well, what do you think?' she asked.

'I think ...,' he said. 'I think you did **all right!**'

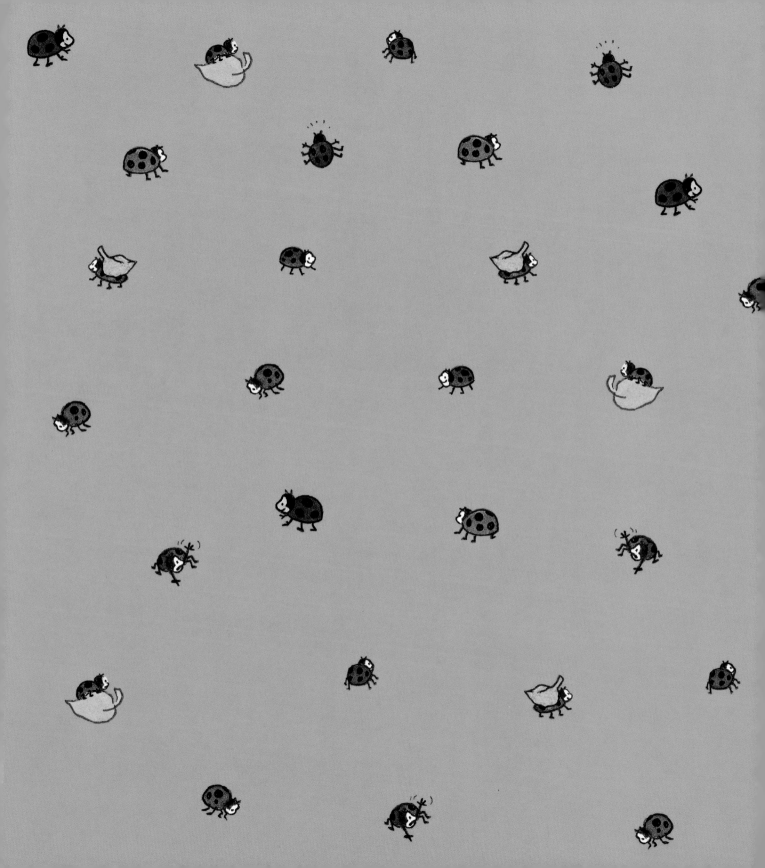

About the author

Bob Darroch has been a freelance cartoonist and illustrator for a number of years. He started writing and illustrating his own books for children in 1999 and released *The Kiwi That Was Scared of the Dark* in 2001 and *The Kiwi That Lost His Mum* in 2002. Bob lives in Temuka and is married with two children and two grandsons.

Other books by Bob Darroch
*   The Kiwi That Lost His Mum
*   Little Kiwi Meets a Monster
*   The Kiwi that was Scared of the Dark
*   Te Kiwi Mataku i te pō
*   The Tree
*   Is it Time to Get Up Yet?
*   Little Kiwi Looks After the Egg

REED